The Evenness of Things

Deborah Jenkins

The characters and modern day events of this book are
entirely fictional.

To Mum and Dad

With love

Thank you for all the stories

X

The Evenness of Things

A woman drives a car in sunshine. In the back young adults snore, plugged into things that end with "pod" or "pad". The car whisks through villages, stops at lights. On a corner a young couple embrace. She wonders briefly if it is a first love. It occurs to her that she has fallen in love twice: once with a vicar in a pub in Greenford – she didn't realise he was a vicar until it was too late – and now, twenty-two years later, with a house. These two fallings have more in common than you might suppose, with Mark in recovery on both occasions; the first time from a Communion Service in which his cassock caught fire on the paschal candle and the bishop's wife fainted. Daisy thinks of his face, smouldering in dim light near the bar, long fingers clasping a pint like a prayer. He needed rescuing and she, fresh from teacher training and a job offer, had gladly obliged. In the end they had rescued each other and the arrangement had been so mutually beneficial that they had married and kept it going until The Thing. After that there was no question of rescue for either of them ever again.

This time the recovery is from a hernia operation. Mark is a reluctant patient – an *impatient* – and since the operation was in July, she'd decided when term ended to take him away to recuperate. Today was a beach day. As she helps him swing his legs through the car door and down onto the driveway, she decides rather unfairly that she herself would quite like a chance to recuperate – preferably from a condition that requires her to be cooked for and lie down a lot. Something gynaecological perhaps, or a nervous breakdown. Pulling the beach bags from the back of the car and barking at the kids to help because Dad can't, she decides that a nervous breakdown would do nicely.

As she locks the car and turns to the house, she is filled with pleasure for the fifth day running. Generous stone, and through sash windows a glimpse of garden. The front door is open, beach bags dumped on stone flagged floor, and beyond the porch, the heavy banisters of a sweeping staircase. She walks, supporting Mark, into the cool darkness, running her eye along the pleasing lines of lintel and cornice. She'd known, she'd just known, the minute she'd seen it, that the house would save her. All that searching and clicking on endless photos, googling round 'til her brain hurt; it had paid off. Why so many beautiful holiday lets – honey coloured stone, leafy garden – are filled with seventies' furniture and Formica, is beyond her. Who goes to these places? What's the point of a stunning exterior, when the interior is like the before section on a DIY shoot? But then beauty matters to her. It always has. It soothes her. It gives her hope. There is little beauty in her life these days since The Thing so she grasps for it wherever possible and always on holiday.

So she'd kept looking. It had taken every evening that spring at the dining table guarded by marked books in neat towers like watchmen, with the garden beyond bathed in lemon coloured light. It was quite late to be looking and there had been so much rubbish that she'd almost despaired. Finally she'd clicked on The Dower House. It was beautiful – sash windows, pillared porch and long limbed trees cradling the house with leaves. Breathless, she'd clicked on rooms, the garden. There were two lounges, one with TV, a large kitchen, conservatory. Upstairs, several bedrooms, and outside a huge garden full of trees and wrought iron. She'd clicked on the location, her breath rising with desire. Alnwick in Northumberland, close to the coast, Lindisfarne. And the week she'd wanted was the only one available. It was everything she'd hoped for. And it had been there all along. Waiting...

She eases Mark into the conservatory and goes to boil the kettle. The kids disappear. She wanders round the kitchen smoothing oak, assembling mugs. It is so quiet here, a million miles from the concrete fields, the rat race – a retreat. She opens the kitchen door. Beyond the trees the light deepens and shadows nip at the lawn with cool fingers. There's the heady scent of clematis, the sound of doves.

Daisy is tired after a day on the beach, but she's drawn outside into scented dusk. She pauses, breathes, walks along the wall to the gate. She hears the kettle gurgle and click behind her, glimpses Mark dozing behind sun-drenched glass. The air has that seared-earth smell of summer, of timelessness. It reminds her of being young, when the world is full of hope. She stands for a moment at the back of the house, admires the rise of stone, the trees. She should go back and spoon tea but she doesn't. The future, she decides, even now is full of unmined potential. She watches herself return to the kitchen and make drinks, a patient woman in her forties resigned to carrying on, looking after things. But on a whim, she doesn't follow. Instead she goes after the other woman, the one who walks to the end of the wall, through the gate and into the lane. And the woman in the kitchen, the impassive vicar's wife, whom she has carefully put on every morning for over twenty years, evaporates like thin mist, a puff of smoke.

Daisy wanders unsteadily between hedges. She feels drunk. In a way she is drunk, plump with the intoxicating scents of summer, unhinged by beauty. There is birdsong, trees, cottages hunched together like cats. The sky blushes shy of nightfall and the light pales and drifts. In the distance church bells peal across pleated fields. She wonders if she can face the close of the week – the coming to terms with the end, the slow retreat, gathering, packing, parting. She imagines the last glimpse of stone flagged hall and stairs as she swings the heavy door shut; as she reverses the car, a glimpse of garden through sash windows. She thinks of driving to London, of arriving at the vicarage – an ugly box with a flat roof – and it makes her want to cry. It brings back the memories, after all these years…

The town begins abruptly – the castle first, proud towers thrusting above the river and, behind, the ancient stone buildings of Alnwick. She passes the walled garden, the castle entrance. There are tourists spilling out with rucksacks or children and carrier bags from the castle gift shop. They are talking about the time, what to have for tea. She feels a stab of guilt. Mark will be awake and thirsty. The kids will be hungry. It will not occur to anyone that they could do anything about this. She pushes the thought away. There is a greedy pleasure in roaming the streets of the town at dusk when she should be back getting supper.

She wanders cobbled streets, drawn down alleys narrow as limbs. There are lighted windows, glimpses of things –

family meal, woman on phone, old man reading. He suddenly looks up and sees her and their eyes meet through dimpled glass. She moves on, embarrassed, wondering if he's here on holiday. He looks too relaxed, too rooted to be here for a week. But then she was like that at the start. It's only today, she thinks, as the end draws in, that she's filled with sadness.

She emerges from the alley and walks towards the market place. Here the shops are closed and the pubs and restaurants are filling with people. She pauses for a moment and reads the menu at The Alnwick Arms, assessing whether they could afford it on the last night. A waiter approaches from within. She does not notice him until two crisp triangles of bow tie hover by her face.

"Can I help you, Madam?" he begins, but she steps away quickly, swaying slightly, and looks intently into the window of a nearby estate agent. Out of the corner of her eye, she sees him smile and incline his head before returning to his post inside the door. She breathes. And then, she sees it.

The Dower House, Alnwick. The photo is picked out in tiny lights. She peers closer, recognising the curved driveway, sweep of stone. Her eyes swivel to the top of the poster. She cannot believe the price. She breathes. Could they have left off some zeros? A house like that! It's not possible! But this is the north, another country where life is slower, cheaper.

The estate agent is still open. There are two couples inside, both seated on leather chairs talking to agents. Daisy squints between glossy stills of holiday homes and beach huts. A blonde lady in a white suit and sunglasses rises from one of the seats and extends her hand, smiling. She drops a document into her clutch bag – a flash of red nails and jewellery – and then she and her companion turn to leave, looking pleased. Perhaps at this very moment they are closing a deal on The Dower House. Daisy feels a clutch of fear. Although she'd be losing something she has never owned, the house is part of her now. It has opened a door wedged tight with the sticking plaster of years, ever since the day when everything changed.

There are steps up to the entrance of Sanderson Young, Estate Agents and Property Consultants. Daisy waits until the blonde lady and her companion have negotiated the door and are back on the street, the lady slow in stiletto mules. Then she climbs the steps, pushes the door, goes in.

***

The last day of the holiday is to be spent at Holy Island. Lindisfarne. She rolls the word on her tongue like a spell. For Daisy it will slow the creeping tick of time, as she has been looking forward to this for months. Who can resist an island castle reached by a road through the sea? They drive across early while the tide is out, a distant stretch of blue on silver. The sky is huge, swallowing the car with easy gulps as the land ebbs, and they are surrounded by mudflats. The air is pure salt. Seabirds on pipe cleaner legs turn heads and stare in lazy-slow light. There's the buzz of a boat.

"Daisy! Watch the road!" Mark is anxious. He twitches towards the steering, a nervous passenger, preferring to drive, to be in control.

"I'm fine, just looking. Don't worry!" She doesn't blame him. She is easily distracted and prone to sudden manoeuvres, preferring to look, to admire.

Even the kids are impressed, searching the sky, wires disengaged, devices unplugged. In the mirror they look like returning astronauts. She smiles at them.

"Do you like it?"

"Yeah!" says Chris, "it's awesome!"

"Where's the castle?" Tom's hair is still sleep-tousled.

Jack looks punch-drunk. He yawns.

"Wait 'til we get there. It's on the other side. That's awesome too!" Chris smiles. With a rush, she realises he's looking so like…

"Mum!" they all shout in surround-sound. She is dangerously close to the road's edge. She swerves, regains control, breathes, flushes. Mark exhales. Out of the corner of her eye she sees he is gripping the seat as if at Thorpe Park.

"For Go…goodness sake Daisy! Watch the road!" She has only ever heard him swear once. He had been trying to repair her bike in the sitting room of her tiny flat in Greenford, his hand in the wheel, patiently checking, adjusting. She had been sitting on the saddle watching, fascinated. He had leaned back on his heels, she had thought he'd finished. Riding a bike across the carpet of a small sitting room is challenging enough without the complication of a hand in the wheel. He had shouted, really shouted and a stream of unrepeatable expletives had issued forth from those sermon-preaching lips. Even she had been shocked – but later, as she lay beneath the heavy blankets of her maiden bed, she had decided that it made her want him more. He was a vicar but a human one. His outburst proved that most of the time he was able to master the emotions that derail most people. If his composure had grown stronger over the years, she was glad.

No longer did she take pleasure in his easy smile. It reminded her of Rosie.

The anger builds inside her as they drive on in silence.

11

The engine drones, a curlew dives screaming into the marshes. She, having organised this holiday, having planned and packed and plotted routes and driven everywhere, makes one mistake and the whole family bellows. A barrage of male outrage. She inhales.

"I made a mistake, okay?!" She looks sideways at Mark's profile; the set face, the patient jawline. "Just give me a break! You know I hate driving…and I've had to drive *everywhere*!"

He says nothing. He never rises, reacts. He thinks everything through carefully, too carefully. She coughs, irritated.

His voice, when he speaks, is patient. "You know I'd rather be driving, but I have no choice! You've done well to do it all. Everyone makes mistakes, don't let it ruin the day. I know how much you've been looking forward to it." He turns to her and smiles, the effort apparent in his demeanour, the lines about his mouth. But his eyes are kind, she notes. This is not easy for him either. The familiar guilt rises, heats the back of her neck like a scarf. She sighs.

"Mum?" Chris touches her shoulder, her soul-mate, her baby. "It's cool, okay? Relax – it's your day." And it's true. They have a day each on holiday, control of all decisions – where to go, what to eat: five days and two for travelling. It has worked for years.

And it will work today. She shrugs, nods her head, gives a small smile. Mark touches her hand. They park in a car-park by the village with a view of the sea. But then everywhere on the island fronts the curve of sea and sky. From the inn to the gift shop to the Priory, the vista unrolls in painted indigo. It calms her. It fills her with hope. She walks with Chris, his hand tucked in her arm, exclaiming at the stillness, the light. Tom supports Mark, walking slowly, careful of his stitches. Jack, the zoology student, is last of all, wielding binoculars and a camera. They wander between shops, visit the scriptorium where Daisy marvels at the pictures inked in vibrant hues. One catches her eye – a dove with outstretched wings against a rainbow. The text, penned in blue and gold, is familiar: "Do not let your heart be troubled. And do not be afraid." The ancient words she's been brought up with – Sunday School, Youth Club, church twice a week – stir memories of another life, safe, secure…

She turns away.

"Let's go to the castle!"

They walk along the winding road towards the jagged tooth of whinstone that is Bebloe Crag, topped by the fairy-tale fortress. Huge birds stretch, snow-lined wings angled to the sky. The sea purrs and gleams on the right while on the left the land sweeps wild, a saltmarsh with scrubby grass criss-crossed by walls. She cannot take her eyes from the landmark at the end of the road with its square towers and narrow windows. She turns to wait for Mark, smiling.

"Isn't it beautiful?" she exclaims. "Imagine living there!"

Mark is walking more normally. She watches him swing one leg in front of the other, without wincing. His hair needs cutting, she notices. It curls below his ears, reminding her of the other Mark, the younger, carefree one. The holiday must have done him good. He reaches her, smiles back. "I knew you'd love it."

They walk together, a family group among groups – couples, kids, parents with buggies and picnics.

"Don't go too close to the edge!" shouts a young mum with pigtails. Her son keeps running, looking over his shoulder with delight. She swears audibly, throws down her rucksack, gives chase. "Daniel! DANIEL! Come here!

One…two…"

Daisy recognises the desperation in her voice, the angst. The curse of motherhood, the daily onslaught of anticipated dangers that could snatch your child away in seconds. Don't worry, she wants to call after the swinging pigtails, it doesn't make any difference in the end. They will survive or they won't. There is nothing you can do. The young mum reaches the boy and swings him up into her arms. He is chuckling, his mouth square and pink like a wound. She relents, buries her face in his neck, blows bubbles. He looks about four. Daisy abruptly pushes away a memory – soft curls and chubbiness, the delighted laugh of capture. She breathes, turns her face to her son.

"Can you read it?" she says, shoving the guidebook at Chris. "I left my glasses."

The history of Lindisfarne Castle fascinates her – the Tudor Fort, protecting the last English harbour from the Scots. Then the garrison, naval store, coast-guard station. But the best bit, the part that chimes like a bell clear and pure within her is when a tourist goes for a walk, finds a castle, falls in love. She makes Chris stop and show her his picture. Edward Hudson, founder of Country Life magazine. She stares at the black and white photo – craggy face, hat lowered over pale eyes, dreamer's eyes.

"*'He had grown up in a drab villa in Notting Hill and had the city dweller's idealised view of country life,'*" Chris reads. Daisy listens, thinks of the discovering, the dreaming, the joy of acquisition – a place like this, a slab of stone between sea and sky, a refuge. Buying and renovating must have been a dream come true. Then the slow realisation – too far from London, too draining, too expensive. She imagines having to sell after three years, after all that work to create the perfect sanctuary. A bachelor most of his life, with a prestigious job, a broken engagement, Hudson finally married at the age of seventy-four only to die seven years later. The love of his life was a place.

They arrive at the foot of the crag, climb up, explore. The inside of the castle is stunning – whitewashed walls and antiques. There are brick floors, gleaming brass, blue and white china. It is still a home, as if the owners have just popped out. Admiring the Dutch furniture, the yawning fireplaces, Daisy wonders what makes a house a home.

After they have their fill of vaulted rooms and stone corridors, they sit on the upper battery, a vast roof terrace flanked by a cannon and incredible views. From here they can see the harbour, the mainland, a ribbon of sand arcing towards Bamburgh. And the ruined priory. Her eyes run across its jagged outline, the haunt of holy men like Aidan and Cuthbert. A place of peace dismantled by Henry VIII, its stone used to build this castle. Life, she thinks, has a way of evening things – a people's priory, a place of hospitality and prayer, torn down by a greedy king. A fortress built, a castle home, a dissatisfied owner chasing a dream. Then eventually, in 1944, a gift to the National Trust, restored to the people again.

"Cool view!" Jack slings his arm round her neck, extends his binoculars. She can feel the strength of him, the hard muscle. She turns her head, smiles into his eyes. Her boy, her going-to-be married man. He tilts his precious binoculars. "Mum, look!" The view is dazzling – a clutch of houses, a gash of sea and near the flats, hundreds of seals sunning on sapphire.

"Seals!" she exclaims. She can hear his smile.

"I told you, huh? Worth a look!"

The young, she thinks, are masters of understatement.

"Wow! It's amazing!" They bob, carried in frisking

waves, unselfconscious, free…

"Have you seen the seals?"

Mark turns from his vantage point at the battery wall, flanked by the other two.

"What seals?"

"Oh! Here, look!"

They love the seals. Tom wants to take one home. Chris wants to stuff one. Jack wants a wall-sized picture for Carrie.

"She loves seals. She practically is one." They laugh, think of Jack's swimmer fiancée, her muscled body, sleek hair. Such a pity she couldn't come with them this year.

They leave, walk back towards the village. Daisy's one regret is there's no time to visit the Priory.

"It's just a ruin, a pile of stones," moans Chris. She meets Mark's eyes.

"I'd like to see it too," Mark says, "but it is late. We can't miss the tide. We spent too long up there…" He jerks his head towards the receding pile of volcanic rock and its magical castle. Too late. She has always loved the atmosphere of holy places. This one a ruin, light-bursts through stone. A place of pilgrimage, even today. She sighs. Too bad.

The journey home is slow. There are no sudden manoeuvres, no lapses. The sun lowers on pewter coloured sea. The birds have nested, the tide turns. The holiday is within a whisker of ending. Tonight, fish and chips, packing – the habits of years. The young adults sleep. Even Mark dozes, reassured by her slowness, her deliberation. She thinks of the house, of that which she has set in motion, and wonders with a curious detachment, as if considering another's actions, if it will save her after all.

**

They drive away in morning light, the house dissolving in wing mirror view, but she is warm with knowing. Her father's money, left to her, banked in her name – he would have loved this. She looks sideways at Mark, wonders what he will say, what he will do, when he finds out. The thought of it gives her a jolt, a frisson of fear. He mustn't find out.

Back in London, she unpacks, tidies, moves around the house like a robot. It is not her home any more. It's just the vicarage, a place where she lives. Her home, her real home is at this moment being acquired by an agent, a wide hipped house with casement windows and buff coloured stone. Sun in the kitchen – on the floor clean squares of light. She thinks of the curving driveway, the wide rooms. She has asked them to negotiate for the furniture, the fittings. She wants everything. She will have it.

The rest of the summer, when she sleeps, she dreams of generous rooms and tiled chimney breasts. Mark heals, goes back to work. The boys come and go. She puts the holiday photos on the computer, the house her wallpaper. When the agent rings, or the bank, she takes the call upstairs or outside. The evenings are long, brooding. London bakes beneath fan oven skies. Carrie comes to stay. She is good company – cheerful, helpful, though Daisy sometimes catches her watching, as if unsure of her in some way. Daisy is warm, reassuring. She knows she could not have chosen better for her boy. They have so much in common, they are true friends. This is a good loss, not like the other.

Papers come in the post for her to sign. She tells Mark they are to do with her father's money, different accounts, interest options. He nods, relieved she is taking care of it. He is not a money person, has no interest, spends little.

17

"We'll have to start talking soon," he observes, "about what to do with it, where to buy."

She stiffens, tightens with guilt, apprehension. She clears her throat.

"Are we going to buy?" Her voice comes out a thin squeak, like a child.

Mark starts. "I thought that's what you wanted!" he says, frowning.

She colours. "Well, yes. I thought that's what I wanted..." She stops, considers, feels the web of lies constricting her throat like a noose.

What has she done?

"But then there's uni fees for Chris, so much higher now. Maybe we should save it for..."

"Daisy, we've been through this!" He's becoming impatient. She recognises that look. *I don't know where I am with you.* Neither do I, she thinks wildly, neither do I.

"We'll talk about this later!" Mark says, dark with displeasure. He makes for his office, slams the door. She breathes. It hits her. What has she done?

The next few days are dreadful, a nightmare of her own making. Every phone call, every envelope, she ignores until she can no longer bear the possibility of Mark finding out and rushes headlong, skidding to the letter box, the phone. How long can she keep this up? She delays the solicitor, questions the survey. One day she is going to stop it all, stop it now. The next, she is filled with longing, for the space, the silence. She cannot sleep. She has palpitations. It's Rosie dying over again. But this time, it is her fault, not his. She must talk, to someone.

***

Sunday is one of those freak October days. The sun is blazing by nine. The papers trumpet that it's hotter than Ibiza. Inside the church the air is hazy. The pews, polished to a slippery gleam by S.I.C.C. (the Sanctuary Internal Care Committee), smell of beeswax. Daisy smiles at Lorella, Mark's right-hand woman, a New Zealander whose defining characteristics are her height and vast quantities of lipstick. Lorella smiles redly back and Daisy thinks for the thousandth time that you could not find a more unlikely church warden if you invented one. The church is full – families, older people, the man from the corner shop. They sit there in the drowsy warmth, still and staring or chatting to each other in hushed tones, as if God is noise-sensitive.

Daisy makes her way to the front pew, nodding and smiling as she does so. She greets a newcomer, chucks a baby under the chin. The stained glass windows are flooded with sunshine and the altar is bathed in light. Daisy looks at the cross, not the shiny one on the altar but the wooden one Mark has placed on the steps below. She prefers this one – old, rough, lurching a little, like people do, like life does. *I need to talk to you,* she says to the God of her upbringing. *I'm not coping with the Rosie thing any more. I need you to help me.* Dust motes somersault in the warm air. She sits, waiting for that old, safe feeling that whatever has happened or will happen, God has some kind of master-plan. She can relax into life again, knowing that in the end, everything will come right. She looks up. The cross just stands there – crooked, empty. Nothing.

***

Anna's fork freezes en route to her mouth. By the counter a waitress drops a dish. There is a small scream. Heads swivel, turn back. She stares at Daisy.

"You *bought* it?! What do you mean, you *bought* it? Is it too late? Can you give it back? Daisy, what are you *doing?*"

"I don't know." Her voice is quiet, her eyes down. "I think, I think, maybe...I'm having some kind of breakdown..."

She has said it, said it out loud, unpeeled the mask which has coped with unspeakable tragedy and moved on.

There is a beat. Anna's voice is low, urgent. "You *must* see someone, talk to someone. Daisy, you *must!*"

"I'm talking to you, aren't I?"

"I don't mean *me!* Daisy, you know what I mean! Someone...professional." She pauses before the word, afraid of it.

"What? You mean a counsellor, a psychologist, a *shrink*..." She feels her head jerk up, her eyes blaze.

"Daisy, for God's sake!" There is a pause. "You're a vicar's wife! You've probably urged others to do this, arranged it for them, even."

Daisy wipes her eyes with the back of her hand. She feels the brush of her lashes, cool and dry. What Anna doesn't understand is, she can do this for others, support them in crises, arrange counselling. But she cannot do it for herself. She just can't, because then the floodgates would open. And everything, *everything* would gush out, the pain, the anger against Mark, against God. It would destroy her. It would destroy them all. Doesn't her best friend, her old schoolmate, understand?

But Anna looks back at her with earnest eyes. She is flushed, concerned. Anna with her three children, all grown, all *alive* – straightforward husband, Hampstead home. How could she possibly understand? She has never had to suffer anything. And she probably thinks that fourteen years is long enough to get over a death, even the death of a child. A memory – the counselling arranged for them, the sallow face of the big-boned man behind his desk, asking questions that neither she nor Mark could answer, imprisoned in their shock, their grief. It was too much, too soon. For a split second she allows herself to imagine telling someone now, about that day in June – her return from work, the smell of heat, the sun-baked tarmac. The back view of a little girl, singing....

"No!" She brings her hand down on the table, hard. Anna jumps. People look, stare.

"I'm sorry. I'm sorry, Anna!" She rises awkwardly, jogs the table. Her latte spills in frothy whorls. They spread across her plate like flowers. She feels hot, unsteady.

Other people lose interest, look away, resume talking about the weather, the cat.

"I...I have to go."

She goes.

***

She buys the house. She cannot see a way out. There is no way out, she is in too deep. The money is paid, so is the agent. The letters stop, school starts. She and Mark settle down into their old rhythms – cooking, eating, keeping clean. There is no more talk of the money. The two students return to uni, driven by a recovered Mark in a car stuffed with guitars and jumpers. Chris studies in the kitchen while she cooks. They chat, exchange funnies. She helps him with his A Level French. She has another year of him yet – a whole year. The little girl from long ago stops singing, sleeps...

The season stills, the air cools. She co-ordinates the

collection for Harvest. Church stuff…

There is a local authority review at school. Daisy prepares lessons, marks too quickly – *"Great characterisation! Well done. I love "diaphanous" but not sure it's a word. It is a word! Sorry! Just looked it up! Most impressive!*

Please reread piece and put in two full stops and a question mark."

The review passes. Half term approaches. She texts Tom. "Are you body at half term? Could I come and visa?" Tom lives in a messy, shared house with three other lads, but they are laid back, friendly. She has hosted them in London.

She hears back from Tom that evening. "How are you getting on with your new phone Mum?! No I'm not BUSY and would love you to VISIT!"

Daisy plans the trip carefully. She'll stay at the house and go to Tom's for two days at the end. She relies on Mark's workaholic tendencies and the fact that his church warden is in New Zealand, while Chris will want to be in London with his friends.

"No, that's fine, you go…" Mark wipes his plate carefully, with a wedge of potato, "I'll get a load done while you're away. Will they want you there for the whole week though?"

"Well…I thought I might pop in on my brother on the way…"

"Okay." He rises, late for a church meeting, kisses her uncharacteristically. "You'll enjoy the break. You deserve it…"

As the door slams, silence flows into the spaces left by him – the study, the lounge, the chair left at an angle pointing away from her. Somewhere far away there is the low throb of Chris's music.

Is it really this easy to lie to the person closest to you? But perhaps that's the thing, she thinks, absently scraping fat into the food waste. We aren't that close, any more.

***

She drives in rain, on tyres that hiss. The cars in front are cubicles of warmth. Blurred women stretch and yawn and talk at men. Children wave. She grips the steering wheel as the road ribbons between towns or trees. Driving makes her feel purposeful because, at least for now, she's going somewhere. She sighs, filled with rare pleasure by the pastel coloured fields. Beyond the road pale hills bruise the horizon and the sun lowers on coppered trees. She pulls off the motorway as daylight fades and Eddie Mair wishes her a pleasant evening. The town is greyer than she remembers and the wind has picked up. An empty crisp packet somersaults across the road. Someone has closed the gate to the house so she has to pull off the road and park. As she slams the car door, her heart thuds in her chest like a drill. This is her house – the first house she has ever owned. Nothing can touch her here. The wide rooms with their high ceilings, the garden, the antiques; all these have been waiting for her these long months, preening themselves quietly for her arrival, just beyond the double gates. She hastily texts Mark. "Am here. All well."

Once she's opened up and driven in, the word that comes to mind is "naked". The trees, imposing in summer, seem frail without leaves, pale branches lifting-lazy like tired limbs. The drive is covered with leaves and the paint on the front door Is peeling. She expects this. The house is not looked after and kept tidy for tourists any more, and she has

23

not organised maintenance in her absence. But it is worse, much worse than she anticipated. As the front door swings open, she is assaulted by the smell of decay, and cold. The air in the hallway with its tiled floor and immense height is freezing, far colder than outside. Daisy shivers, opens the drawing room door. She doesn't even know how to work the central heating. There's a dead mouse in the middle of the carpet and one of the heavy curtains sags on a broken rail. There's the smell of damp. In the kitchen she knows there will be no Welcome! Basket with home-made biscuits and different teas, but she does not expect the dead plants and assorted crockery. There's even a breakfast bowl in the sink ringed with congealed cereal. How had she not realised that the owners would remove their beautiful dining ware and saucepans?

Filled with dread, she slowly explores the rest of the house. She checks the conservatory. Damp wicker furniture and dust lines on shelves. The garden is overgrown, huge thistles thrusting through dirt, the sweep of lawn overgrown. The hallway with its imposing staircase smells musty and the view from the arched window is hung with cobwebs. There's mould on the bathroom wall and a patch of damp where a laundry basket used to be. Everywhere, the sense of papered over cracks, disguised for tourists, emerging with knowing smiles. She wrenches open the bathroom window and stares, dismayed, at the unkempt garden, realising her face is wet. How stupid and delusional can you be? And how could she ever have thought that she could recapture a sun-filled holiday, in cold October?

She washes her face. The water is brown and smells of rust. She doesn't care. She is tired after her drive and the familiar despair at her madness, her ability to self-deceive, is overwhelming. But even as she is filled with self-disgust, at the back of her mind is an awareness of the need for heat, for food. She has a memory of Mark opening a cupboard in the master bedroom and saying something about a weird place for a boiler. She stares at the pale woman in the mirror – wild eyed and dripping – then wipes her face on a piece of toilet roll. The main bedroom door is closed. She has to grasp the beautiful painted handle and push hard. It's only as she manages to yank the door open that she realises there is something behind it – an empty bag of some sort. The large room is dark and she feels briefly disorientated. She strides across to the window and hauls at the curtains before remembering the curtain pulls. The heavy material swishes across the bay and she turns to examine the beautiful four poster bed. Just as the person in it sits up.

Time tumbles. They stare, appalled. For a wild moment Daisy thinks she recognises her. *Why? Why would she think this?* The girl, she thinks it's a girl, is tousled and sleepy. She rubs her eyes with her knuckles as if she could still be dreaming. Daisy feels a surge of emotions but the overriding one is white hot anger.

"What the hell are you doing here, in *my house*?" Her heart is skipping but her voice is cold and tight. Part of her brain registers the fact that in no part of her uncertain scheme of things has this house ever belonged to anyone but her. Obscurely she thinks of her wedding vows, *"With this ring, I thee wed, and with all my worldly goods I thee endow."*

"Oh my God!" It seems to dawn on the girl what's going on, "Are…are you the owner?"

"Yes, I am the owner! And I'm going to call the police!" The new mobile feels slippery in her hand as she tugs it from the pocket of her jeans. She's not even sure how to use it. She holds it up and jabs randomly.

"Oh please! Please don't!" The girl pushes at the covers and leaps out of bed. She must only be about seventeen or eighteen, thinks Daisy, taking in the strappy top, the bony shoulders. She has short hair, huge eyes. "I…I can explain!" she says, and bursts into tears.

Daisy's lungs deflate like old balloons. She sighs. She does not feel equipped to deal with this situation. She has had a long journey, a hard arrival, a shock. She can't cope with a distraught teenager as well. She suddenly feels incredibly tired. The immediate threat is over – the girl does not look dangerous, or armed. She is just some sort of a squatter, albeit a rather well-spoken one. The girl has begun to shake. The air in the bedroom, now that the huge windows are uncovered, is bitter. Daisy picks up a thick dressing gown from the end of the bed and hands it to her.

"Look," she says neutrally, "I'm sure we can sort this out. Do you…" She pauses, takes in the neat pile of folded clothes, the hot water bottle, "Do you know how to turn the heating on?"

***

Her name is Jude, she lives in Alnwick. She left school in the summer and works at Barter Books. She tells Daisy this with a certain pride. Daisy is relieved. Barter Books is the stunning second hand bookshop she spent hours in last summer, based in the old station. Surely anyone who works there must be…respectable? Half her brain laughs uncontrollably at this. *How can you judge what is respectable?*

"I pay my own way. I don't rely on anyone!" Jude says, then colours, remembering her current predicament, "I mean, usually," she adds.

Daisy nods, and waits. They've turned on the heating, been shopping, prepared food. What strikes her most is the seeming normality of it all; a middle-aged woman, a teenager, a shopping trolley with sticky wheels, a till assistant with acne; Jude carrying the shopping basket and, later, cooking pasta drenched in sun dried tomatoes. Her hands are small and light as a bird. Daisy lifts the Asda wine glass to her lips and feels the warm red glow easing knots in her shoulders, her neck. She considers her new friend – small, self-contained, marching round Asda suggesting bread, some cereal.

"I don't live here," says Jude. She has been watching her, Daisy realises, in between bites. "I just come here sometimes, when…when it all gets too much."

Daisy has a lurch of recognition. "Me too," she murmurs. She pours some more wine.

"Actually, it used to be our house before…before you bought it." Jude announces this quite matter of factly, though her voice trembles a little at the end.

"Really?" Daisy puts her glass down, missing the mat. It lists drunkenly and some drops of wine spatter the plate like blood, "What, like last summer, when we rented it?"

When Jude's eyes light up, she looks quite pretty, not like the gender-less creature that rolled out of bed earlier.

"Did you rent it? Were you the family with all the boys?" She looks excited, eager. In spite of herself, Daisy laughs.

"Yes! All the boys – that's us!" She raises her glass, "Why? Were you spying on us?"

"Maybe…a bit!"

Daisy frowns. She had thought the girl looked familiar, or maybe she'd seen her in Barter Books. God knows, she'd spent long enough in there.

"So…why did you sell it?" Daisy feels a wave of

tiredness sweep over her but she is determined to find out more about this girl, this stranger, before she surrenders to sleep.

Jude looks down at her plate. Her neck, Daisy notices, is so smooth and vulnerable, a young person's neck. Mine, she thinks regretfully, used to look like that. She plucks at it now, the rough flaps, the aging skin.

"My…my mother died." It is a simple statement, spoken quietly, without self-pity. It is a fact, thinks Daisy, that people die. Mothers, children, old people. Everyone, really.

"I…I'm sorry…"

There's a beat. The boiler gives a sudden whine, then clicks back to life. There's a flash of headlights – a car in the lane.

Jude is still examining her plate. With a fingertip, she draws circles with smears of tomato. Her nails are thin and pointed like claws. "She…she ran the business, you know, sorted the house, dealt with the agent. Dad couldn't cope when she went. When I was younger, we lived here, you know…" She glances up at Daisy and nods at her raised eyebrows. "Then when Dad retired we moved out, bought somewhere smaller in town. It broke my heart…"

"I…I can understand that." Daisy hopes her words aren't slurred; she's very tired now. "To have a beautiful home like this, then to give it up. I would hate that…" She thinks of Edward Hudson, of falling in love with a place. What would Beblowe Crag be like at this time of year? Briefly she imagines Hudson visiting it in winter, mounting the ramp, standing in wind-folded darkness with waves crashing on the rocks below.

"I live with Dad," continues Jude. She smiles and her face is filled with warmth. "He's lovely. He doesn't know I come here – he thinks I'm staying with friends. He just texts to make sure I'm okay…He used to be a vicar, you know."

"Ah, a vicar…" Daisy runs aching fingers through her hair. They always hurt after a long drive. Mark says she holds the steering wheel too tight. A good description of her.

On impulse, she reaches out gently and touches the girl's cheek. "My husband's a vicar," she says. "It's good to know there's life beyond vicar-ing. What does your Dad do now?" Her hand drops to the table. "I must go to bed soon," she mutters to no one in particular, "I'm shattered."

"He's a counsellor," says Jude. She gulps her wine, mouth wide as a baby bird. "He helps people deal with bereavement."

***

Daisy feels a strange sense of deja-vu as they walk together, a tall woman, a slim girl, walking close as if they've known each other all their lives. There is an ease, Daisy thinks, in Jude's company that she has not felt with a young woman before. Usually they scare her, teenage girls – their confidence, their skin, the awareness of impact. She has brought up boys, understands their humour, their directness. The space reserved for the little girl from the past was never filled, its shape unknown. *What would she have been like?* Would she have been like this, she wonders – independent, unafraid?

They leave the house by the garden gate and walk between fields to the town. She remembers that evening last summer, the heat, the drifting light. Today the light is naked, the trees bare-armed brown. It's still early and the cottages are quiet, their windows lazy-eyed. A cat washes paws on a wall. There's the smell of smoke. It's hard to believe this is the same route that she walked four months ago leaving a kettle boiling, wandering out, buying a house. Even now she cannot believe it. What had she been hoping to achieve? As they round a bend in the lane, there's the peal of bells. She had forgotten it was Sunday. Mark will be laying out his notes, adjusting his cassock. She has spoken to him, checked he's okay. He has asked after Tom and she has answered automatically, the lies coming so naturally it scares her. *Tom's popped out for milk. He's fine though. Carrie's here. She's cooking. He sends his love. Hope you're okay.*

When they get to the castle, Jude sighs. "I love this place."

Daisy smiles. "It is beautiful," she agrees, "a fairy-tale castle. Not for the real world."

Jude glances up at her, grins. "But it is the real world!" she says. "Some fairy tales are true!"

There is a beat. I cannot believe, thinks Daisy, after all you've been through, that you still believe in fairy tales. But that is just me, she decides, because I know that my fairy tale, the one I've been writing for the past few months, is about to implode. And I don't know if I'm ready...

"So it seems..." she says.

Jude's father lives in a tall house off a narrow alley in the market place. It has taken all of Jude's persuasive powers to convince her to see him, and even now she is aware of the thin line between going and not going. *Daisy, you must talk to someone*, Anna had said. Would talking to someone change anything now? And what would she say to a man who she's meeting through a squatter daughter he knows nothing about?

"I'll tell him we met at the book shop," Jude says firmly, "and realised the connection with the house...and got talking."

When they arrive at his house and Jude leans up to push her key in the lock, Daisy remembers wandering down here last summer, the lighted windows, the glimpses. *A touch of madness...* If she could only rewind her life, go back to that evening – stand in the garden fringed with heat and silence – she would follow the first woman, the one who went back into the kitchen and shut the door. The one who made tea and took it to her husband in the conservatory and then sat with him, reading or dreaming in the warmth of the evening. They might even have talked, the way people do, of how wonderful it would be to own a house like this, a house that you could rent out and escape to yourself when you'd had enough of things. They might even have googled and looked at prices and dreamed a little longer, before deciding reluctantly that the idea was exciting but impractical, given the busyness of their lives, the distance from London. Most people, she thinks, as the door swings open, dream the dream. That is all. Apart from her, and Hudson. *But if we're going to turn the clock back, let's turn it back altogether. Let's get rid of The Thing completely. Let's stop all of this before it ever started.*

Jude's father is called Robert and has sharp eyes that see the heart of things. Daisy shifts uncomfortably in the arm chair which is trying to swallow her whole. The room is warm and she feels drowsy in a patch of sunshine. The book-lined walls, she notices with a housewife's eye, are impeccably organised and dust-free. There's the smell of polished leather. The silence is beginning to unnerve her. They have made their introductions, Jude has proudly explained that her Dad is the best when it comes to counselling. Alnwick, she gushes, is full of former basket cases now living the life of Reilly because of her Dad.

"Jude!" Robert frowns, but he touches his daughter's face, ruffles her hair. Daisy can't help thinking that he may have failed when it comes to Jude, whose grief at her mother's death drives her to break into their former home in order to feel close to her. She, on the other hand, has always wanted to run away from the place where Rosie died, the garden where she sang and dug in the sand, the swing…

Robert is sitting, watching her. He is older than she'd thought, wearing half-moon glasses and a quizzical expression. When he eventually speaks, his voice is gravelly, his manner detached, but the image he uses jolts her into wakefulness.

"Grief," he observes, "is like a house we build over time. My job is to help you work out what you've built so you can begin to understand it…"

Daisy gives a small laugh. "That's interesting." She tries not to sound cynical but fails. "A house! Very apt, in my case. Is that why you chose it?"

He keeps watching her. The checked collar of his shirt, she notices, is tucked neatly under his jumper which is navy with leather elbow patches. All very trim, very tasteful. Perhaps this is how you deal with grief, she thinks. You sanitise it, tuck it in at the edges, then use your new-found tidiness to help others.

He ignores her question, but gives her a small smile which causes his face to crinkle. It makes him kinder. "Why don't you just talk?" he says. "And I will listen."

Daisy laughs again, nervous. "What shall I talk about? Where do I start?"

He shifts and settles in his arm chair. His manner is calm, unhurried. "Just start at the beginning," he says.

Daisy is still walking the *I might stay/I might go* line. She could easily get up, thank him, say after all, this was not for her. She could wish him and Jude well, walk out of their lives. She doesn't owe them a thing. On the contrary! (She can see the exclamation mark in her head.) Back at the house, she could tidy up, change the locks. Nothing was making her stay here and open her soul to this stranger. It is a moment, she thinks, like the one in the garden, where everything could change, or nothing. The silence stretches. Robert waits. Time. She looks down at her feet. They lie next to each other loosely, ankles crossed. She moves the left one a little so they look symmetrical, even.

In her head, a memory. Rosie's plump feet, Rosie's voice, clear as a bell, explaining as they walk up the stairs, "If I miss a step and put *this* foot on *that* step, I have to miss a step again, for the other foot. You know, Mummy? To be fair to my feet…"

Daisy draws breath. The voice is so clear, it's as if she's actually heard it. She uncrosses her ankles.

Her voice, when it comes, is unfamiliar, quieter, more tentative. It is the person that she hides from the world, the one who is unsure of things, the child.

"It happened in the summer," she says, "A hot summer's day, in London, fourteen years ago…"

***

Tom looks worried. "Mum, are you okay? You look tired."

She sets down her case, gives Tom her coat, embraces him. "I'm fine, darling. Don't worry about me. A long drive, lots of traffic." She has forgotten how small Tom's terrace is and half of her brain is registering that it looks somehow different – lighter, cosier, stuffed with cushions and prints. It was a long drive but she knows this is not why she is tired. Her day with Robert left her punch-drunk with exhaustion, and all she has wanted to do since then is sleep. He warned her it would be this way but she had had no inkling of just how much. She had slept for two days at the house, spent two more days on cleaning and DIY, then yawned all the way down the M6. Parting from Jude, in front of the old station at Barter Books, had been strangely emotional.

"I have never met anyone like you my whole life!" Jude's eyes had flickered briefly in her small face. "You could have had me arrested!"

"Well, I did try." Daisy smiled. "Probably I would have, if I'd known how to work my phone!"

They hugged. And when she drove away, girl waving in wing mirror, a key to the house was safe in Jude's pocket and the first month's cleaning money tucked in her purse. And she was smiling.

Tom's world pulls her in quickly, too quickly. It takes her five minutes to work out that, since she and Mark visited Sheffield last spring, Tom's three mates have moved out and Carrie has moved in. She greets her son's fiancée warmly, aware of her nervousness. She admires the change in the house, the feminine touch.

"You've made it into a home!" She smiles. "When did you move in? Tom, why didn't you tell us, darling?"

Tom has sat down. He has his arm round Carrie and he's looking embarrassed. "I know. I know, Mum. I'm so sorry." He runs his fingers through his hair – long curls she wants to touch. Her boy, her man-boy. "We wanted to, but we were so worried about what you and Dad would say. I know what you think, what you believe, about these things. We were trying to give ourselves time, to work out how to tell you. And then…and then, we just ran out…"

"Is this…is this why Carrie didn't come with us, in the summer?"

Carrie nods. "I wanted to tell you!" she says. "I wanted to tell you after, when I felt better, when I came to stay…but it was…it was so hard…"

"Yes," says Daisy, "I suppose it was." And now, she thinks, you have waited long enough to save yourself the trouble. Because you are now very clearly, very obviously, pregnant.

***

Mark is pleased to see her. You would not be, she cannot help thinking, you would not be if you knew all the things I have to tell you.

"It's great to have you home! I've missed you!"

She is surprised. He never says this kind of thing, is never needy for her, never emotional. He carries her case indoors, makes tea, sits on the edge of the sofa.

"So tell me, tell me about Tom. Did you see Carrie? How's it all going?"

She is so tired. In her mind a procession of cars, and motorway signs, and wrung out tissues, and a pregnant woman or two. "Mark, darling, would you mind? I'm so tired. Could I…could I give you all their news, tomorrow?"

"Of course!" He leaps up. "Come and eat, then you can go to bed. Chris is out. Look, I've got it all ready!"

She sees he has laid the table, bought flowers. He has even tried, clumsily, to arrange serviettes in goblets, lit candles.

"This is lovely!" She is touched. He smiles as he serves a casserole, gleaming with generosity, excitement at her pleasure. It makes her want to cry.

In the end she doesn't wait until morning. Mellowed by alcohol, by his kindness, she decides maybe the time is now.

After all, they haven't talked for ages. For years, really…

***

Mark swills wine. The colours reflect light from candle and lamp. The fan oven purrs and clicks. There's the smell of coffee. She breathes, looks at him, breathes again.

"So…we're to be grandparents?"

He looks, if not pleased, at least interested by the thought. Her lungs relax. She remembers that you don't have to think about breathing most of the time. It just happens.

"Not, not how we'd hoped it would happen, I suppose…?" she suggests tentatively.

He considers. "No." His eyes look green in the lamplight. Most of his face is in shadow but his temple, the gentle flat of it – the curve, the heart of the man – is tipped towards her. She wants to touch it. Her fingers itch to feel its softness, its vulnerability. But she can't, yet… "But then, much of life can be like that, can't it?" He looks at her then. "Things happen. We don't want them to, but they happen anyway…"

Her heart begins to thud. He has done this before, tried to talk, to open things up and she has backed away. For fourteen years she has backed away, because it's been easier. Jude's father had not said much but what he'd said mattered. *You cannot deal with another's pain but you must deal with your own.* And she'd realised suddenly that since that day, her life had been one elaborate attempt to avoid pain. She can feel it now, the length and breadth of it, the heaviness of it, lying on her stomach like a slab.

"I…I…" With a rush she wonders if she actually can speak of it, even if she wants to, so ingrained is the habit of years. He is watching her intently, leaning forward, eager. The familiar sick feeling squirms in the pit of her stomach, the flustered resistance, pushing away the memory of that day. Her senses have always betrayed her, the imprint of tragedy a clean impression, the sounds and smells stamped indelibly on nerve endings. She prepares as usual to heave them away. *What do you think is going to happen?* Jude's father had asked her. *If you let yourself go back, what's the worst that can happen? The worst has happened already...*

She looks at Mark, really looks at him – the quiet expression, the waiting face, expectant, hopeful. It is one of those moments, she thinks, where everything could change, or nothing. But then life is full of such moments. You just don't know which ones they are, until after. She breathes out slowly and a ripple of air and memory sails across the space between them. And he catches it.

There's smell of burning tar in her nostrils, the shimmer of heat. The air con isn't working and the windows are jammed low. London is cooking slowly – a mass of barbecued flesh and beer – lurching through the last days of July. As she pulls into her road, there are people standing at their front gates, talking, holding bottles or ice-creams. Londoners coming out to congratulate and commiserate. "Aren't we lucky?" "Could do with some rain though," "The poor gardens!" It's that kind of small-house road, where people come out and chat, unlike the big-house driveways and restraint that she was brought up with. As she slows, filling with the Relief of Home, she waves at Mel-across-the-road through the passenger window. Mel is young and blonde with a tattoo and a two year old. She waves back, her daughter anchored to her hip.

Daisy's house swims into focus. The square vicarage with its ugly roof looks a bit better since she's planted up pots, started a path. She can see that Mark's left the front door open – it will be stifling in the house today. As she turns the wheel to pull over, she glimpses the bob of blonde heads and it fills her with pleasure. Her twins, her babies, digging in the sand ready for the paving in the front garden. Blonde curls, fat necks bent over buckets, beaded with sweat, Rosie singing as she mixes brown sand and earth, "Pat-a-cake, pat-a-cake, baker's man..." The thought of scooping them up, the smell of their skin, lips on dimpled arms. The gate is shut, they're safe. These are the last things she remembers thinking.

It happens quickly. For months she cannot understand this, the speed of it – how a single second can be the dividing line between something and nothing. One second. It is such a tiny thing, most of the time unremarkable. A lifetime is filled with two and a half billion such seconds. How is it possible that only one can render the other two billion, four hundred and ninety-nine million, nine hundred and ninety-nine thousand, nine hundred and ninety-nine completely and utterly meaningless?

A click of the gate, a crunch, a soft thud. Then the sound of the engine, louder, different than usual. Later, she is told that neighbours screamed and Mel ran and Mark rushed through the door, dripping with sweat, dropping his phone. But she doesn't see any of this. She just sees a thin blur in a tiny sundress, running towards the car, arms outstretched. And somehow, just somehow if she stays exactly where she is, hands clamped to the wheel, head on the horn, she won't lose her.

After she's been peeled away from the car and the police have come, and the neighbours have gone, and the doctor has injected her with a needle so long and sharp that she wonders if she will be impaled on it – night falls. And she turns her face to the wall. And she no longer has a daughter, only sons…

***

When she's finished, she realises they're no longer at the table but on the sofa in each other's arms, and the candles have burned low and smell of charcoal. They are holding each other so close – she across his knees, his arms around her like a baby – that she can't tell if she is making his face wet or the other way round. They do not sob. There have been years of sobbing, not together but alone, in the park, in the garden, with others. Anywhere but together, in the house. But now there are words – quiet and wet, not accusing. Sad. Factual.

"I'm always distracted when I'm driving. If only I hadn't waved at Mel…"

"I went in for a minute, *one minute,* to answer my phone. I was walking out with it, talking. If only I'd been there, I could have shouted…"

"I've blamed you for that for fourteen years. Because I couldn't face the truth about myself…"

"I've watched you, suffering and cold, and I've wanted so much to tell you…it was *nobody's fault.* She just got up, and ran."

"But if I'd slowed down earlier, if I hadn't waved, if I'd not been thinking about other things…"

"A tragic accident. That's what the courts said. Remember?"

"Then, why? Why did God let it happen?"

She's been wanting to ask him the question for so long that when she does, it hangs in the air like a noose. And she is scared of it.

"Daisy." His hands are in her hair, his lips on her skin. "I don't…I don't know…"

His voice is so quiet, she can hardly hear it. "*Life can only be understood backwards, but it must be lived forwards.*' Kirkegaard… That," he sighs, "is our tragedy. You have coped all these years by blaming me. I've coped by working too hard and too long. We have to change, find another way…"

Another way. "Yes," she breathes.

The last candle flickers and dies. It's late. They've not even closed the curtains. There's a slice of vanilla moon rocking high up in the darkness. The wall they have built between them, she thinks, is coming down. Perhaps soon anything will be possible again. She puts her face as close to him as she can, feels the warmth of him, the solidity. And the weight of The Thing, the slab of sorrow anchoring her to that July day, begins to shift, to crumble a bit. And for the first time in years, lying in Mark's arms, Daisy has that old safe feeling that somehow, somewhere, everything will be alright. In the end…

Later, in bed, she's almost asleep when Chris comes in to say hello. He's embarrassed. "Oh! Sorry – didn't know you were here, Dad!"

Mark nods awkwardly. Chris has probably never seen them like this, in the same bed.

"Come kiss me, Chris darling…"

He leans down, rubs her cheek with his stubble. She squeals.

"Do you ever feel…?" The start of it is out before she has time to think, but she doesn't care. It doesn't matter any more. "Do you ever feel that you're half of a whole?"

Chris flinches. They do not discuss this. It is taboo. He looks down at her, then across at Mark, then up at the photo of two blonde children on the beach in Cornwall. Sensing something – a shift, new rules – his face softens. He has the look of his father, she thinks, the strong nose, concave temple.

"No, Mum," he says. "I can honestly say I've never felt like that. I don't remember her like you do. I was only three…"

She smiles. "Yes, of course."

"Goodnight, Mum."

"Goodnight, Chris. And darling…" The door is almost closed. He pokes his head through like a mole.

"Yes?"

"I'm glad…"

***

It is so late and she is so tired that she has slept and woken and slept again before she realises that he has been lying awake for hours, on his side, watching her.

"Mark, you need to sleep. You've got work tomorrow."

"I'm watching you, checking, that you're alright."

"I'm alright. But Mark – there's something else…"

"Mm, hm?"

"I did a bad thing."

"A bad thing?" He's stroking her face, her hair. She props herself up.

"No, Mark you must listen. It's the last thing, the last thing. Between us."

He stops stroking. Waits. Outside, a couple of inebriated youths exchange expletives. The distant rumble of a bus. Then silence.

"I…I bought a house." She stops, examines his face. He looks straight back at her, doesn't flinch.

41

"The one we stayed in last summer. I…I don't know why I did it. I just…needed somewhere beautiful, a retreat…"

When he speaks, it's very soft, almost a whisper. "A retreat?"

"A…a place where I could be quiet, somewhere beautiful…I saw it in an estate agent and I…I had a moment of madness…and I bought it, with Dad's money."

Mark's face is so serious that she wants to cry out. She is fully awake now.

She cries out. "Mark! I'm sorry! I'm so sorry! I can't explain what happened. The secrecy of it killed me! I so wanted, needed to tell you!"

He looks down then straight at her. "I know."

Shock fizzes up her spine like a shot. "What do you mean? You know?"

"I know about the house." He's still speaking quietly, almost dreamily. "Daisy, I'm not an idiot! You were always rushing to the phone, the letter box. I knew something was up…"

People know more than you think... Jude's father had even known about his daughter's squatting habits.

But how can you let her? Daisy had been outraged. *She's breaking the law!*

Jude's father had shrugged. *She's not hurting anyone, is she? The house is empty. And it's helping her, giving her a place to recover, to heal…If you throw her out, you throw her out.*

She hadn't.

"How did you find out?" Her voice sounds small and squeaky, like a child.

Mark sighs. "Daisy, you work, remember? One day I opened a letter and made a phone call. It wasn't hard."

A small silence. "Did you…were you angry?"

A small laugh, wrinkling his eyes. "I wasn't thrilled, Daisy! Your Dad's money, our money – gone, with no discussion at all. Yes, I was angry. But later, I began to understand – you needed somewhere, somewhere to run to. After all you've been through, I could hardly deny you that…"

Relief floods through her, making her skin prickle. "Why…why didn't you tell me?"

He rubs his nose. His nails are short, square. "I wanted you to tell me, when you were ready. And you have…"

She nods. "Didn't…weren't you worried when I went away?"

"No." He leans back, easing his shoulder. "I was just relieved you were alright." He's lying on his back, very still, but she can feel him watching her. "I was glad you were seeing someone."

"*What*?!" She sits up, turns, leans over him. "What do you mean?"

"I was glad you went to Robert Armstrong."

She knows her voice is too loud, for three o'clock in the morning. *"How do you know about Robert?!"*

"Shh!" He clamps his hand over her mouth. "You're too loud! I…I hired someone, to check on you…"

She can feel her eyes blazing. She pushes his hand away. Her breath smells stale and old. She'd been too tired to clean her teeth. "You had me *followed*?!"

Now he's the loud one. "Daisy! You bought a *house*!" They're sitting opposite each other on the bed – crumpled sheets and whiffs of wine and sharp bursts of breath. "You bought a house and you didn't tell me! I was worried about you! I had no idea what you were doing up there! I rang Tom, of course – I knew you must be in Alnwick, on your own. I knew you weren't well, mentally well, so I had you

43

followed. I was so relieved you were seeing him! Robert's well respected in Anglican circles. He used to be a priest – he's a fantastic counsellor."

"Yes, I *know* he's a fantastic counsellor! That's probably why we're talking like this in the first place…after all these years! You have your Anglican Robert to thank for that! Where would we be without you amazing Anglicans?!"

Silence. The breath of an impasse. But she knows, with all that they've been through, there must never be an impasse ever again. She reaches out to touch his face with her finger. "I'm sorry about the house, Mark!"

He catches her finger in hands that tremble, kisses it. "It's okay."

They lean into each other, moving in the way they used to before they slept alone. Before The Thing that parted them.

And afterwards, replete in each other's arms, she whispers, "We'll sell the house!"

She thinks at first he has fallen asleep. Eventually he whispers back, but now he cannot tell if she sleeps, her chest rising and falling evenly like a child. Like the child they once lost, and who was perhaps, finally, leaving them in peace again.

"Maybe," he says. "Maybe…"

***

A woman drives a car in winter. In the back, there are songs and laughter and the smell of cheese. Behind them the boot is stuffed with food and drink and clothes from Asda. She can hear bottles of Prosecco clinking. It makes her smile. They whisk through villages, stop at lights. On a corner there is a Christmas tree covered in angel hair. She wonders what happens when it rains. Perhaps angels don't worry about their hair. Little shops line village streets, their windows strung with tinsel and coloured lights. The day is fading and there's a hint of snow – a few wandering flakes floating lazy-slow down.

It is hard to believe, she thinks, that two years have passed since they left London, three since the all-nighter with Mark. She hasn't thought much about Rosie for ages. And when she does, it's about those three years with her rather than the lost seventeen. She still keeps a running total in her head though. It will always hurt, she thinks, watching a young mum drag a tiny child across the road in front of her. Fronds of blonde hair loop out of a red hood and duffel coat far too big for her. Perhaps this, she wonders, as the thick material almost brushes the tarmac, is why she is howling, her mouth wide open to the sky. She reminds Daisy of an overweight robin.

The road to Alnwick is swallowed up in minutes. As they arrive she rolls the name of it around her tongue, tasting it. The Dower House. Swinging into the drive, she has the same thrill she first had when they arrived for their holiday from London. Sash windows, mellow stone, trees. The car crunches on gravel as she curves to park by the old wall. The front of the house is festive with the door wreath and tiny lights.

The girls tumble out, crowing over Chris's sudden appearance at the front door, Jack and Tom behind him. Daisy's heart turns over. Her boy, her baby, home from university. Carrie shouts and Rosanna runs. Chris swings her high up and round, tosses her to her father. She squeals. Daisy follows slowly, drinking it all in – her boys, her daughter-in-law, her grand-daughter.

Chris hugs her. "Hey, Mum!" But he's looking over his

shoulder towards the car. Daisy smiles, because she's known all along since the first day Chris met her, he would only ever have eyes for Jude.

They all grab bags. In the end she doesn't need to carry anything. She tidies the seats, rakes out crumbs, locks the car. The front door of the house is open. Through the kitchen window she can see Mark directing unpacking. The door to the drawing room's ajar – a square of lamplight, a fire. She pauses.

Of course a house cannot save you, she knows that. But in the right circumstances – peaceful, beautiful, with trained people like Mark and Robert for support – it can help. Beauty is so important, she thinks. It soothes people. It gives them hope. If she had been able to go to a place like this all those years ago, perhaps she would not have suffered so hard and so long. But then if she'd found such a place, they might not be here now.

"Hurry up, Dais!" Mark is shouting. "You're letting the cold in!"

From the kitchen, there's the sound of protest, of laughter.

She steps inside and her eye falls on the crib scene in the hall. She feels guilty, closing at Christmas – a bad time for so many. But, as Robert keeps reminding her, even people who run Retreat Houses need retreats.

Life has a way of evening things. If you let it. If you listen.

She drops her keys on the table and goes to join the fray.

Thanks to Mary Fleeson of Lindisfarne Scriptorium for permission to use details of her inspirational artwork
www.lindisfarnescriptorium.co.uk

Thanks also to Penelope Swithinbank for a soul restoring retreat weekend during which much of this story was written.
penelopeswithinbank.com

Deborah Jenkins is a freelance writer and teacher, who loves hats, trees and small children. She is married to Steve with whom she has two grown-up children and a cat called Oliver. Her full length novel, Braver, will be published in the summer of 2022 and tells a story of unlikely friendships and heartbreaking decisions. Deborah blogs at **stillwonderinghere.net**.

You can follow her on Twitter @loverofhats

Printed in Great Britain
by Amazon

35127197R00029